9/16

# MOO

# SHARON CREECH

# MOO

JOANNA COTLER BOOKS
*An Imprint of HarperCollinsPublishers*

Library of Congress Control Number: 2015952544

ISBN 978-0-06-241524-0 (trade bdg.) — ISBN 978-0-06-241525-7 (lib. bdg.)

Typography by Ellice M. Lee

16  17  18  19  20    CG/RRDH    10  9  8  7  6  5  4  3  2  1

First Edition

*For*

*Karin, Mark, Pearl and Nico*

*with special thanks to*

*Pearl, Greta and Audrey*

*and all the*

*dedicated*

*4-H-ers*

*at*

*Aldermere Farm*


*and to their intrepid leader,*

*Heidi*

# CONTENTS

## THAT ZORA

The truth is, she was ornery and stubborn, wouldn't listen to *a n y b o d y*, and selfish beyond selfish, and filthy, caked with mud and dust, and moody: you'd better watch it or she'd knock you flat.

That's Zora I'm talking about. Nobody wanted anything to do with her.

Zora: that cow.

## BUT FIRST, BEFORE ZORA . . .

I am Reena, twelve years and two months old,
formerly of a big city, a city of monuments,
and people of many colors, a harlequin city
of sights and noises,
of museums and parks and music
and cockroaches and rats
and mosquitoes and crickets
and fireworks and traffic
and helicopters whopping overhead
and sirens *screaming* through the air
and that's how we lived for a time

2

me and my parents and brother
zzzooooooooommmmming
on the

      subway

or creeeeeping along in buses or cars
in
   to
     and
        around
           the city

trawling through the museums
   *ogling*
the dinosaurs and artifacts

ambling through the zoo
listening to the ROARS and SCREEEEEECHES
and scrabbles and warbles
staring at the l a z y  crawls

of bored animals.

Yes, for a time that's how we lived.

## FLIGHT PATH

Then one day, when we were stuck in traffic
behind a tall gray bus spewing exhaust
with horns HONKing
and people YELLing
and sirens WAILing—

on a day that was hotter than hotter than HOT
my mother asked my father a question.

A question can swirl your world.

My parents had recently lost their jobs when the newspaper they worked for went out of business. We were on our way to drop my father off at another job interview.

*So,* my mother said, *do you still like reporting?*

*Not so much,* my father admitted.

*Is that what you see yourself doing ten years from now?*

*Um—*

*Because that's the flight path we're on.*

I was sitting in the backseat with my brother, Luke, a seven-year-old complexity. Sometimes he acted as if he were two, and sometimes twelve. He was full of questions and energy and opinions except when you wanted him to have any of those things.

Luke was drawing with a black marker in the yellow notebook that was nearly always with him. He drew for hours and hours: contorted heroes leaping and jumping and vaporizing; bizarre enemies with gaping mouths and sharp talons and horns; and complicated towns with alleys and bridges and dungeons.

In the car, when Mom said, *Because that's the flight path we're on,* Luke said, *Flight path? We're not in an airplane, you know. We're in a* car *and we're on a road,* but I noticed that he was adding a runway and an airplane to his drawing.

Drivers all around us were HONKing their horns like crazy, and the smells and the heat and the NOISE were pouring in the windows and

**squeezing** us

from all sides.

7

*Let's get out of here,* my mother said.

My father took his hands off the wheel and raised his palms to the sky.

*No, I mean out of this city,* my mother said. *Let's move.*

*To——?*

*Maine!* I said.

My parents turned to look at me.
Then they looked at each other.
Then they looked at me again.

*Maine!* they said. *Of course!*

My parents had met in Maine many years ago and when they spoke of Maine
their voices had the glint of sea and sky.

In the car that day,
*Maine* just popped out of my head.

I hadn't expected they would take me
*seriously*.

I'm glad I didn't say *Siberia*.

## WHICH IS HOW . . .

Which is how I came to meet Zora, though not quite so easily as it might sound because first we had to give our landlord a month's notice and then we had to clear out all our closets and cupboards and the dreaded storage garage. Then we had to lug some of that outside for a yard sale and the rest to the Salvation Army and then we had to clean and watch as future renters tromped through our rooms noting

how small they were and how old
and how dark and
it
was
embarrassing.

And then there was the packing and moving of
the beds and clothes and books and pots and
pans—oh, it hurts my head to remember it so
let's skip it.

## PEOPLE SAID . . .

My parents' friends said
*Are you crazy?*
and
*It gets cold in Maine, you know.*
and
*There are giant mosquitoes in Maine.*
and
*It gets cold in Maine, you know.*
and
*Why? Why? Why?*

12

But some others said
*They have lots of lobsters there.*
and
*Great blueberries in Maine!*
and
*Beautiful ocean and mountains!*
and
*Great skiing!*
and
*Lots of lobsters!*
*Lots of blueberries!*

*Though . . . it does get cold there*
*you know?*

Luke said
*How did this happen*
*this moving thing?*

In his yellow notebook
Luke drew a winged dragon

scaled in gold
flying through purple skies
grasping a house, a car,
beds, tables, and chairs
in its black talons.

## WHY MAINE?

Why did I say *Maine!* that day?
*Let's move to Maine!*
Because I'd read a book about it—
three books in fact:
two were stories about a family's life
on an island in Maine
and one was a book of photographs
of rocky shores and lighthouses
and vast oceans with breaking waves
and high blue mountains
and while I was reading those books

and looking at those pictures
I was there already
in my mind.

I was clambering over rocks
and wading in the ocean.
I was hiking up a mountain
and standing at the top
peering down the steep hillsides
to the ocean beyond.

I was there.

Maine.
It had such a *sound* to it
such a feel.

And yet . . .
I'd always lived in the city
I was full of buses and subways
and traffic and tall buildings

and crowds of people
and city noises
        honking and sirens and
        helicopterwhirring
and city smells
        bakeries and car exhaust
        hot dogs and coffee
and city lights so bright . . .

Was there room inside for
the sights and sounds and smells
of
Maine?

Would I know what to do
and how to be
in
Maine?

## FRIEND WITHDRAWAL

The few friends I had didn't believe me when I told them we were moving to Maine, and then when I'd convinced them, they acted excited about it, but as the days went by, I realized they were already forgetting me. It seemed they didn't want to waste friend effort on someone who was leaving town.

One of them said, *You're going to get all Maine-y.*

I wasn't sure what "all Maine-y" meant, but

whatever it was, they had decided it was undesirable.

My parents had similar reactions from their friends. At first people thought they were joking, and then they seemed excited and curious, but gradually they became less and less interested.

My mother was hurt by that, but my father said, *Maybe they're jealous or maybe they feel you're abandoning them.*

When Luke told his latest friend, Toonie, that we were moving to Maine and that it was far away and he couldn't come over to her house anymore, she socked him on the nose and called him a *stupid doofy head.*

When Luke told Dad about his encounter with Toonie, Dad said, *Well, who knows, maybe we're all stupid doofy heads.*

# WELCOME TO MAINE

With that white chalky paint
that newlyweds write
*Just Married*
on their cars
we wrote
*Moving to Maine!*

And all along the way
as cars and trucks passed us
people honked their horns and waved.
Some rolled down their windows

and shouted: *Maine!*
and some scribbled signs
and held them up for us to see:
> *Eat some lobstah for me!*
and
> *I love Maine!*
and
> *We're so jealous!*
but one guy's sign read
> *It's COLD there!*

At the border
we pulled over and posed beside
the WELCOME TO MAINE sign.
People honked their horns like crazy
as they sped past us.

Maine!

In a small town three hours up the coast
we parked by the post office

and walked to a diner for lunch
and when we returned there was a note
on our windshield:

*Welcome to Maine!*
*We hope you like it here.*

The ocean was a block away—
you could smell that salty air.
People were walking their dogs
and their kids
and the church bells were chiming
and the sky was blue.

Maine!

Dad stepped in dog poop
that oozed into every crevice
of his running shoes
but still:
*Maine!* We'd made it!

## HARBOR TOWN

It was the beginning of summer
and we thought we'd landed on another planet:
a boat-bobbing
sea salty harbor town
with people strolling the docks
eating ice cream and lobster rolls.

Gentle mountains rose up opposite the harbor
and curled around it
wrapping the town
in their bluegreen embrace.

*How exactly did we get here?* Luke said.
He drew towering mountains
and steep cliffs
above jagged rocks
and tiny, fragile boats
bobbing in the ocean below.

We made our way
to the place my parents had rented:
a small old house
with a woodstove inside
and an apple tree outside
and a chipmunk on the doorstep
and a chickadee nest in a lilac tree
and spiders in the woodpile.

That same day our parents said
*Go on, ride your bikes.*
*Check out the town.*
*We've got unpacking to do.*
*Go!*

*What?* we said. *By ourselves?*

In the city where we'd lived
there were few safe places
for us to ride—
few places where we weren't competing
with cars and trucks and buses
and surprise clumps of kids
armed with sticks and stones
or wobbly bearded men spitting

but here in this little town by the sea
there were wide sidewalks
and quiet, curving lanes
spreading like tree limbs
from the trunk of the town center
and you could ride and ride
the whole day long.

We rode down streets and trails
discovering our new town

its people and dogs and old houses
its winding lanes and gnarled trees.
One day we passed a farm
and Luke shouted, *Oreo cows!*

Black-and-white cows
(black in front and back
with a wide white fur belt)
munched at the grass.

A girl about my age
in rubber boots
stood near us
on the other side of the fence.

*Belted Galloways, they're called,*
she said.
*Or just Belties, for short.*
*Purty, right?*

## A COW

Maybe I had imagined a cow was like a
LARGE lamb:
soft, furry, gentle, uttering sweet
sounds.
But oh—
not so, not so!

One of the Belted Galloways
lumbered up to the fence
and pushed its
        ENORMOUS HEAD

with its

ENORMOUS NOSE

toward us and uttered a

DEEP DEEP LOUD

*MOOOOO*

so loud and deep as if it were

coming from low down in the ground

and traveling up through the cow's legs

and body and head and out of that

ENORMOUS

SLOBBERY

MOUTH:

*MOOOOO*

so LOUD and surprising that we

j u m p e d     back

and the girl in the rubber boots

gave us a pitying look

as if she were thinking

*Silly tourists!*

And I wanted to say

*No, no, we're not tourists!*

*We* live *here now!*

More cows ambled up to the fence
nudging their
ENORMOUS HEADS AND NOSES
between the wires of the fence
and bellowing the
DEEPEST LOUDEST
*MOOOOOS.*

Luke's hands were pressed tight against his
ears.
Flies
     dipped
        here         there
           and

        amid the smell of
          *cow dung.*

## THE FARM

Out riding around on our bikes, Luke and I passed that farm nearly every day. On the gate was a blue and white sign:

BIRCHMERE FARM.

I'd never been to a farm before our move to Maine, and I wasn't sure what I thought of this one at first. On sunny days, it looked inviting, with its green pastures and its barns, and cows dotting the hillsides and gathered in the pens. On the first rainy day, though, when Luke and

I stopped by the fence, it looked muddy and sloppy and smelled of sawdust and manure. Flies dogged the animals and the stalls.

Up close, the cows were thick and wide, with heads as big as kegs, and black eyes the size of oranges, and wide sweating nostrils, and they let out loud, low *mooooos*. They scared me, to tell the truth.

A rotating group of teenagers showed up each day to work with the animals. Only a few adults were around, driving tractors or trucks. We watched the teenagers fill feed bins and water buckets and climb fences and tromp through sawdust and lean against cows. Luke often sat on the grass and drew. His heroes, now, took on the look of farmers brandishing halters and conquering giant cow-like creatures.

# THE HOUSE ON TWITCH STREET

Just before you reached the farm
at the far edge of town
at the end of Twitch Street
was a tall, narrow house
that tilted to one side.

Thick, twisted vines crept up
the side of the gray house
around doors and windows
to the chimney top.

The attic window was cracked and open
and from within you could hear
the sound of a flute

high
     and
          light
              and
                    gentle.

Mrs. Falala lived in the house.
Fuh-LA-la is how you say her name.
Most people agreed she had a cow and a pig
but some said she also had a goat
and an alligator and a bear.

Some people said not to bother Mrs. Falala
because she was old.
Others said not to bother her
because she made
     *weird things*
          happen.

One day our father took Luke and me to Mrs.
Falala's house. *Be respectful,* my father said. *No
matter what you hear or see, be respectful to Mrs.
Falala.*

An enormous golden cat
fell straight down from a tree overhead
landing at our feet.
The cat reared back on its hind legs
and bared its teeth and claws
and out of its mouth came a
menacing
     *hisssssssssssss.*

Our father ushered us up the walk.
*Pay no attention,* he said. *It's just a cat.*

A fat black hog lurched into view
from behind the house
and raced toward the cat
squealing all the while
the most unappealing squeal.

34

*Pay no attention,* our father said, urging us
toward the front door.

High above
from the open attic window
floated the delicate melody of a flute
while behind us the hog chased the cat
round and round the yard
and a bright green parrot perched
on the porch and squawked at us
as we climbed the steps
to the door trimmed in vines.

A sign on the door read
      WRONG DOOR—GO TO BACK
and so
dodging the hog and the cat
under the watchful eyes
of the bright green squawking parrot
we obeyed.

A sign on the back door read WHO ARE YOU?

We looked at each other, me and my father
and Luke.

Luke said, *No way. Not going in there. She'll
probably chop us to pieces.*

My father said, *Be respectful.* He knocked.

Around the corner: hog squeal and cat hiss.

A face appeared at the window beside the door:
   a pale
      thin
         old
            wrinkled
               face.

The hog knocked Luke over
and the cat jumped on the hog's back
and as my father and I battled
the hog and the cat

the door opened and

a long

      pale

          thin

              old

                  wrinkled

                      arm

reached out and pulled my brother inside

and my father and I tumbled in after him.

# INSIDE

At the end of the long, thin arm
was Mrs. Falala clutching Luke
and kicking the door shut.

*You eez living?* she asked.
Her voice was unexpected,
full of honey.
*Eez you?*

My father stepped forward.
*Yes, yes, we are, erm, living, yes.*

He handed her two books.
*From my wife,* he said.
*She asked me to bring them to you.*
*You met her, apparently—*
*at the doctor's?*

Mrs. Falala closed one eye.
*And where eez she, this wife?*
*Why she not bring?*
*She eez living, yes?*

*Yes, yes. She had an appointment today,*
*but living, yes, most certainly.*

Mrs. Falala studied the covers of the books.
Down her back trailed a long, white braid
which she flicked like a horse's tail.

*Wrong books,* she said.

*Wrong?*

*Wrong, wrong, wrong!*
She pushed the books back to my father.

She turned to me and Luke.
*And you, who are you? And you?*
When we told her our names
she tapped my forehead.
*Eez peculiar, no? This name* Reena?

Mrs. Falala caught me trying to peer
around her into the room beyond.
She kicked that door closed.
*Eez nothing there. No going in there.*

I glanced at the ceiling, straining to hear
the sound of the flute
but there was silence.

*What you eez looking at?*
*Shoo, shoo, nothing here,*
*good-bye now, go home.*

As we left the house of Mrs. Falala
seagulls white and gray arrived
one by one
and perched on the ridge atop
her house
not just a few
first ten, then twenty, then thirty
or more
until they were lined up
wing to wing
a row of feathered soldiers
guarding her house
and the flute music
high and light
floated from the attic window.

On Luke's arm
where Mrs. Falala had held him
was a pale blue mark
in the shape of a leaf
and in the sky two white clouds

joined to form a flying girl
long white hair trailing behind.

The hog and the cat and parrot were gone.
I listened for them.
What I heard was the faintest

*moo, mooooo.*

# DON'T YOU TOUCH ME

Luke was not fond of animals.
He kept his distance
much as he did with people.

His first spoken sentence was
*Don't you touch me.*
He said it to a lady in the post office
who then looked offended.
*I won't hurt you, cutie pie,*
the woman said.

*Don't you touch me!*

My mother offered a weak apologetic smile.

Luke said it to a grocery clerk
and an elderly man on the sidewalk
and the doctor.

*Don't you touch me.*

He'd point his finger in warning.

My mother reasoned that Luke just did not
like people getting in his face
pinching his cheeks
squeezing his chubby arms
telling him how cute he was.

*Don't you touch me.*

Now that he was older, he rarely said

*Don't you touch me.*
More often, if someone was swooping in
too close, he'd scowl or run off or
say something silly
like
*Nutto head!*
or
*Frog brain!*

*Funny little kid*
people would say.

When Mrs. Falala had snagged Luke's arm
and pulled him inside
his reaction said it all:
      wild, wide-opened eyes
            stiff arms and legs
                  fingers clenched like claws.

Luke wrenched himself away from Mrs. Falala
with the practiced skill of an escape artist.

I know he wanted to say
*Don't you touch me!*
but he didn't.

That night in his yellow notebook
Luke's drawings included a skeletal
towering figure with a snake braid
and sharp metal claws
surrounded by a posse
of enormous hogs and menacing cats.

## BEAT AND ZEP

I was leaning over the fence at the farm
watching a sturdy dark-skinned girl
maneuver a rope halter over the wide head
of a wide cow that protested
*Moo! Mooooo!*
The girl planted her boots in the muck
and angled her hip against the cow's neck
urging the animal toward the rope loop
*Moo-ooo!*

The girl wore orange canvas overalls

and tall black rubber boots
and spoke to the cow all the while:
*Come on, there you go,*
*don't be so stubborn, over here,*
*back it up, this way, you know how.*

Nearby another teen
a tall, lanky redheaded boy
urged another cow out of a stall
coaxing it into a rope halter as well.

The boy called to the girl
*Hey, Beat, I've got this one—*
and she called back
*Okay, Zep, that's good—*
and it made me smile
those names
*Beat* and *Zep*
*Zep* and *Beat*
but when they looked up
and saw me watching

I turned away
embarrassed
I don't know why
and rode off down the hill
down Twitch Street
and past Mrs. Falala's house
where the flute music
drifted from the window
and the parrot squawked on the porch
and somewhere behind or beyond
was that soft *moo, mooooo*
but no hog and no cat that day.

## EMPLOYMENT

Before we moved to Maine, my parents sent out piles of job applications to the coastal towns in which they most hoped to live. One of those applications resulted in a job offer for my mother, teaching English at a private school near this harbor town. Her job would start in September.

*That is perfect!* she said. *It gives us a couple months to get settled first.*

Dad was still looking for a job. He'd been to lots of interviews and was hopeful that one of them would lead to work. He said he wanted to change direction and do something completely different, maybe something out-doors, maybe something with landscaping (he was good at that) or animals (Really? I knew he liked dogs, but that was about it) or painting (houses). He said he was open to anything, though.

*If I can find something even part-time,* he said, *we'll be okay. We'll have enough to pay the rent and put food in our mouths.*

Luke said, *But if you don't find a job, does that mean we won't eat?*

*Hmm.* He turned to Mom. *Honey, we can always eat the children, I guess.*

Luke went white. *Whaa——? Whaa——? Whaat?*

Dad had to spend the next half hour reassuring Luke that he'd been kidding.

## MISTY MORNING


One misty morning Luke and I rode
along a cobbled wall
past a cemetery with tilting headstones
circling around the back side
of Birchmere Farm
with its pond and grass meadows
and graying, mossy fences
and clumps of cows grazing.

*What are they thinking?*
Luke asked.

*Are they happy?*
*Why do they just stand there?*
*Don't their legs hurt*
*standing up all day like that?*

*Moo, mooooo.*
First one, then several in unison.
*Moo, mooooo.*

*What do you think they're saying, Reena?*
*Are they talking to themselves or to us?*

*Maybe,* I said, *they're talking* about *us.*
*Maybe they're saying*
*'Look at those two over there*
*staring at us like that.*
*What are they staring at?'*

*Mooooo.*

In the area by the barn stalls

three cows in halters were tied
to the fence
their heads held high
their necks outstretched.

The redheaded boy named Zep
came up behind us as Luke asked me
*Why are they tied funny like that?*
*Doesn't it hurt their necks?*

*Naw,* Zep said, startling us both.
*It's stretching them*
*getting those muscles strong.*
*Gonna be good show heifers:*
*heads held nice and high,*
*ayuh.*

Zep held his own head high
admiring the heifers
as I stood there
wanting to say something

wanting to keep him there
a little longer
this gangly Zep boy
but no words came out of my mouth.

Zep repeated *ayuh*
and moved on
ducking into the feed room
as we climbed back on our bikes
and rode down the winding road.

Ahead of me, Luke's neck was outstretched
like the heifers
and as he pedaled
he spoke to the retreating cows.

*Moo, mooooo.*

## ROCKS

Never saw so many rocks:
boulders and stones and pebbles
tall as a bus
small as a pea
craggy and rough and speckled
smooth and lumpy
mossy and pocked
　　　piled along
　　　the water's
　　　edge
stacked

in walls

     along the roads

**jutting** out of yards

gray and brown and silver and green

a jumble of rock stone granite

    **vibrating**

you feel the energy

beneath your feet

coming **up** through your toes

and your legs and your spine

and **out** the **top** of your head

    into

      the


      S  <sup>K</sup>  Y

## BACK TO TWITCH STREET

Dad sent us back to Twitch Street
me and Luke
on our own this time
on our bikes
with more books for Mrs. Falala.

*Can't you come with us?* Luke asked.
*She's too scary. She might eat us.*

*Don't be silly,* Dad said.
*You and Reena can handle it.*

*And remember: be respectful.*

Down along Limerock Street
zig right onto Chestnut
knowing the streets now
knowing what leads where
knowing where the big brown dog lives
and the little yappy ones
waving at the life-size bear sculpture
swooping under low branches
along the river wall
up over the hill
with the wide, wide view
  fields and valley and mountains beyond
stop and turn around
look back:
  OCEAN!
    a wide silk of bluesilver
    spotted with treegreen islands
      beneath
    a banner of bluewhite sky

## OCEAN!

We kick off again
round the loop
skidding to a stop
by the tilting house
of Mrs. Falala
with the open attic window
and the

      f l u t e     m u s i c
               drift

                   ing

                         d

                         o

                         w

                         n

and then abruptly stopping.

No pig
no alligator
no parrot.

INSTEAD: : :


fourteen seagulls white and gray
perched on the rooftop
beaks pointed
down
    toward

        a

           longgggggg
             black

              snake

slithering along the gutter
  its head
    dip
      ping
       over the


        E
        D
        G
        E

                    o       v
              b              e
      just       a


              the door.


We froze.
We stared.


Then the door opened inward
and the long, old thin arm
snatched Luke
then me
and yanked us
inside.


*What you was staring at?*
*What you was spying on?*


The voice full of honey
but the words . . . not.

## THE BOOKS

On our second day in our new town, my mother had met Mrs. Falala in the eye doctor's office. My mother had gone there because a sudden, angry red blotch had appeared on one eyeball.

The waiting room was crowded; the wait was long. My mother had been a reporter and could not help asking questions. She would talk with anyone about anything, and people told her things they might not even tell their family or friends. I don't know how willing or unwilling Mrs. Falala was to talk at first, but apparently she did talk, because my mother came away with a great interest in Mrs. Falala.

*She's from Italy,* Mom said, *but met her husband in Africa and lived there for many years and they had no children and they came here to Maine after Mr. Falala's brother visited here and bought the place on Twitch Street and then the brother died and—*

I said, *Wait. You got all that out of sitting in a doctor's waiting room?*

*Yes,* Mom said. *I'm a good asker of questions and a good listener to answers.*

The first books we had taken to Mrs. Falala's house (*wrong books, wrong, wrong, wrong!*) were about drawing:

because Mom must have somehow learned that Mrs. Falala was interested in that and did not know how to use the library.

When we'd returned home with these *wrong* books, my mother said, *Hmm, I'll try again.* This second batch, which she'd also borrowed from the library, included

*The Art of N. C. Wyeth*
*Landscapes of Maine*

When we offered this new batch to Mrs. Falala, she said, *Put on table.* Her neck and her long arm stretched toward the pile. One long, bony finger flipped open the book on top. *Flip, flip,* through several pages. Then she skidded that book off the top and flipped open the next.

*Flip, flip,* through pages. She did not open the third.

*Better,* she said, *but not . . . best.* To one side and then the other, she jerked her head, swishing the long, white braid that hung down her back. She leaned forward, zeroing in on Luke, who was pressed against my side, his thumb lodged between his teeth.

*You get horse teeth that way!* Mrs. Falala said, and with one finger she snapped at his thumb.

*Don't you touch me!* Luke said.

Mrs. Falala snapped at his thumb again. *Horse teeth!*

Luke was quivering, his elbow vibrating against my side, his chin wobbling.

*Horse teeth!*

*Stop it!* I said. *Leave him alone!*

Oh, Mrs. Falala did not like that, not one little bit. She flicked that long braid clear around her head like a whip and glared at me.

*You rude!* she accused. *Out, out! Go!* She flung herself against the door, pushing it open. *Go! Out! Go!*

## WE WENT

We did not wait.

We jumped on our bikes and pedaled across the lawn and down the walk and into the road and round the bend. Luke was leaning so far forward he looked like a turtle splayed out on his bike. We sailed down the hill, and only then, at the bottom, did Luke wave his arm to the side and we pulled over and stopped by the iron bear.

*That lady is a kookoo head!* Luke said. *That lady is a nutto!*

His chin trembled and his shoulders shook.

*It's okay, Lukey, it's okay. She is a nutto! She is a kookoo head!*

We sat by the side of the road until he calmed down.

*Stupid nutto kookoo,* he said. *And I do not have horse teeth!*

*Of course you don't.*

70

## DISRESPECT

News of our adventure made it home before we did. Both Mom and Dad were sitting on the front steps waiting for us. Luke dropped his bike and raced to Mom and buried his head against her shoulder.

*Hm,* Dad said, *seems like you've had an adventure, you two.*

*That lady's a nutto! A kookoo head!* Luke said, before hiding his head again.

Dad patted the step beside him. *Reena? Have a seat.*

And so I told him what had happened, and when I finished he said, *Mrs. Falala phoned here already. Her version is a little different from yours—*

*What? What'd she say? What was different? Honest, that's what happened.*

*Her version is that you were disrespectful.*

## Disrespectful.

This was not a good word in our family.

*But she was so mean to Luke! She was flicking at him and insulting him and—*

Luke sobbed against Mom's shoulder. *We didn't*

*do anything! We were good kids. She said I had horse teeth!*

*She flicked at him. She insulted him.*

Dad nodded. *And you? What did you do then?*

*I told her to stop it. I told her to leave him alone.*

*Your tone of voice——?*

*My tone of voice? I said it like this: I said, 'Stop it! Leave him alone!'*

*Hm.*

*I was disrespectful?*

*Hm.*

*Well, maybe I was, but she was rude, rude, rude.*

## PRICKLY

Mom said, *Not a good way to start, with Mrs.
Falala. My fault, probably, but I didn't realize she
could be so prickly.*

*You go next time,* I said. *You'll see.*

*Good idea, Reena.*

*And Mom?* I added. *Watch out for the hog—*

Luke jumped in. *And the mad cat—*

74

*And the snake—*

*Oh,* Mom said. *Oh, my.*

The next day, Mom went to Mrs. Falala's
                    *by herself.*
No Dad, no me, no Luke
                    *by herself.*

While she was gone, Dad and I unpacked boxes
and Luke drew intense drawings
of frightening creatures
with hog bodies and snake arms
crawling over housetops and dripping from trees
and one tall, lean, wicked-looking woman
with snake hair and
ENORMOUS
TEETH.

Horse teeth, I guess.

## CHARMING

Two hours Mom was gone. When she returned, she said, *Well! Mrs. Falala was perfectly charming!*

Charming? Mrs. Falala?

*And,* Mom continued, *I think we've sorted out that little misunderstanding and I think we can really be helpful to Mrs. Falala now.*

Luke gripped my arm. I'm pretty sure we were both thinking the same thing:

Helpful?
We?

*And at the same time,* Mom added, *Mrs. Falala will be able to see that you two are not normally disrespectful. You'll start tomorrow.*

*Start tomorrow?*
*Start* **what** *tomorrow?*

*Helping.*

*Helping?*

## MELTDOWNS

Luke: *No, no, no, no, not going to kookoo lady's house anymore, no, no, no.*

Mom: *Now, now——*

Me:   *Do we* have *to?*

Mom: *You might actually——*

Luke: *No, no, no, not going, not helping, no, no, no.*

Mom: *Let's see what——*

Me:   *Did you see the snake? The hog? Did Mrs. Falala snap at you?*

Luke: *Awful, horrible, nutto lady——*

Mom: *All right, Luke, Reena. That's enough.*

       *E n o u g h.*

And when Mom says

       *E n o u g h*

in that way, in that tone, that's pretty much the end of the discussion.

**Over and out. Finito!**

## THE NEXT DAY

The next day, we all returned to Mrs. Falala's:
Mom, Dad, Luke, me.

Luke, who had been attached to my arm since
he woke up, was not speaking. Pancakes and
bacon—usually his favorites at breakfast—
did not interest him. Mom's and Dad's
attempts to nudge him into good humor did
not faze him.

I was not in my best form either. I hate it

when my parents volunteer me for something without asking me.

*Of course Reena would be happy to watch Mikey for you,* my mother promised a friend in our old city more than once. *Of course she would.*

No, I would not. Not after the time Mikey handcuffed me to his front porch railing, dumped a bucket of blue paint on me and the porch floor, and screamed bloody murder for a solid hour.

*Of course Reena will help you clear out your garage, Mr. Conklin,* my father promised our old neighbor. *She'd be happy to!*

No, I would not. Nests of mice in the corners. Roaches on the shelves. Moldy boards and spiders and wasps.

*Do Ben's paper route while he's on vacation? Reena could do that. She'd be happy to,* my father promised his boss.

No, I would not, especially since Ben left terrible instructions and I couldn't read the addresses and there were three terrifying dogs on the route and one exceedingly creepy man with no teeth and orange hair and I tripped on a rock and gashed my head and knees and it poured rain and the papers got wet and the people were mad.

But here we were now: me, Luke, Mom, and Dad back at Mrs. Falala's because my mother had volunteered me and Luke *to help.*

To help with *what* we did not know.

## THE BARN

Oh, that sneaky Mrs. Falala, how she
               s    m    i    l    e    d
                       at my parents
such a sweet, sweet
               s    m    i    l    e
and how she put her gnarly fingers together in
a little prayer pose beneath her chin
and how she pouted at me and at Luke
as if we had hurt her feelings—
oh, that sneaky Mrs. Falala.

When Luke and I apologized for our recent "disrespectful" behavior—an apology my parents made us rehearse on our way over to Mrs. Falala's house—Mrs. Falala stared at us for

one

    two

       three

         eternities

or so it seemed
and she said not a word
until finally my mother said
*Now is there something that Reena and Luke can help you with?*

*Yes!* said Mrs. Falala so suddenly and loudly that Luke skittered back against the door and I reached for my father's arm. *Yes! There eez barn first! Come!* Mrs. Falala lunged through the side door, swirling her bony arm like a windmill, ordering us to follow across the scrabbly yard to a small, old, gray barn and into its dark interior and down the aisle that smelled of sawdust and out the other side and around the back to a fenced area that bordered one of the barn stalls.

*There!* said Mrs. Falala, pointing to a dank sawdusty courtyard splotted with smelly cow dung and flies. *To scoop! To shovel!*

*Ah,* Dad said, *you'd like the kids to help you, erm, clean the pen?*

*Yes! To scoop! To shovel!*

I was trying not to gag from the smell. Luke's lower lip was quivering. Mom's hand covered her nose and mouth.

*Well,* Dad said, *that doesn't sound too hard, does it, kids? I'm sure they could help you out, Mrs. Falala. Right, kids? Reena? Luke? Right?*

*Right?* Mom echoed.

Luke pinched my arm and buried his face against my back.

*Right?* Dad said.

I stood up straight. I looked Mrs. Falala in the eye. She blinked innocently and tilted her head daintily to one side, waiting for my answer.

*Right,* I said.

# SCOOP AND SHOVEL

We scooped

    p    i    l    e    s

    i

    l

    e

    s

    of
    C  O  W
    D  U  N  G

we shoveled

we gagged
            we swatted flies        flies
                        flies  flies        flies


Scoop and shovel and
            P  L  O  P
                        into the wheelbarrow
            piles and piles and piles
            i
            l
            e
            s


While my parents and Mrs. Falala
returned to the kitchen
to drink lemonade
in the cool, dry
non-stinky
non-smelly
non-fly-filled
kitchen

and
when Luke and I were finished
we had to wait for Mom and Dad
outside the house
because we were *too smelly*.

Did Mrs. Falala thank me and Luke
for the scooping and shoveling
of the smelly dung?
Did she?

Noop.

What she said as we were leaving was, *Tomorrow!*

Mom and Dad looked up at the sky, taking
a sudden interest in the clouds above. Luke
grabbed ahold of my shirt, tugging at the hem.

*'Tomorrow'?* I said.

Mrs. Falala's bony fingers danced in the air. She tossed her ropy braid from one side to the other. *Tomorrow: cow!* And with that, she backed into her house and closed the door while up on the porch rail the parrot eyed us.

Apparently Luke and I had been volunteered by our parents to "help for a while."

*What does that mean, 'a while'?* I asked. *A couple days? A week? Two weeks? A month?*

*Hmm,* Dad said.
*Hmm,* Mom said.

*And what does Mrs. Falala mean about 'cow!'? What do we know about cows?*

Luke, who had not spoken since we began scooping the cow dung, now said, *We know ZERO about cows.*

*ZERO,* I agreed.

*Perfect opportunity to learn then!* Dad said, with a strained attempt at upbeat optimism. *Right? It sounds like a great Maine-y thing to do. Right, Reena? Right, Lukey?*

## COW!

The next day, we were back at Mrs. Falala's, just me and Luke.

*Surely you don't need us along, right?* Dad had said. *Surely you and Lukey can handle this on your own, right? And remember, be respectful. Right?*

Right, right, right.

All the way over, Luke said, *Don't let her poke*

*me, Reena. Don't let her scold me. Don't let her be mean to me.*

*I will try my best,* I said, but I was wishing that my parents were along so I could say, *Don't let her poke* me; *don't let her scold* me; *don't let her be mean to* me. And then I thought, *Come on, Reena, you are old enough to handle one little old lady.*

Mrs. Falala was waiting for us by the barn, sitting on a hay bale. *First: water!*

So much for pleasantries.

From her hay bale throne, Mrs. Falala barked orders: *Empty bucket! Over there! Fill with water! See hose? Not too much. Not too little. Put it over there. There! Get feed bucket. Not that one! The other one! Take to feed bin. Over there! Fill it*

*up! No, not full-full! Half-full! Put it over there.*
*There! See? There!*

Luke was moving carefully, almost in slow
motion, and after we'd filled up the water and
feed buckets, he stopped and stood still, his
arms straight at his sides. He turned toward
Mrs. Falala and said, *Where is the cow?*

*Cow?* she said. *You think there eez a cow?*

*Yes,* Luke said. *Yesterday you said, 'Tomorrow!*
*Cow!' and today is tomorrow and where is the cow?*

*You are wanting to see cow?*

*He's not being disrespectful, Mrs. Falala,* I said.
*He's just asking—*

*—About cow.*

*Yes.*

*You are wanting to see cow?*

*Yes.*

*Why didn't you say so? Cow over there——see?* Mrs. Falala snaked her arm toward the pasture beyond.

We saw only grass and weeds and fence.

*There——you are not seeing? By bushes.*

In one corner lying beside sprawling bushes was a black lump.

*That lumpy thing?* Luke said.

*Eez not lumpy!* Mrs. Falala replied. *Go see.*

Neither of us moved.

*What? You eez afraid? Of* cow?

*We are not afraid,* I said. *We are—just—cautious.*

*Pah! Afraid! Afraid of cow!* Mrs. Falala tossed her braid from one side to the other. *Afraid of cow!*

*Come on, Luke,* I said. *Come with me.* I opened the pasture gate. *Let's go see this lumpy cow.*

*Eez not lumpy!* Mrs. Falala said.

Halfway across the field, Luke whispered to me: *Is too. Lumpy!*

The lump, we could now see, was definitely a cow, and it wasn't all black. It was one of the Belted Galloways—black on its front and hindquarters and white in the middle—or at least white where it wasn't splattered with mud. It stared at us as we approached, making no movement except an occasional flick of its tail.

*Lumpy old lazy cow,* Luke said.

And then came the sound, the low rumbling from deep inside and the long, drawn-out *Mooooooooo.* Its eyes were as big as apples and its nostrils gaping black caves. *Mooooooooo.*

*Touch it,* Luke said.

*What? Me?* When you have a little brother, you don't want to look weak. I stepped closer to the cow.

*On its head,* Luke said. *Pat its head, Reena.*

Oh, that was one mighty large head. I bet the head alone weighed a hundred pounds.

*It's not used to us, Luke. I don't want to scare the poor thing.*

*Go on, pat its head so it will know we're friendly.*

I leaned closer and quickly patted the top of its head. *There, there, cow. Hi, there, cow.* The fur was softer than I expected.

Abruptly, the cow tossed its head and let out another lone, low, *Moooooooooo.*

We headed back to the gate, maybe a little faster than we had come. I could see Mrs. Falala watching us, but she said nothing about our encounter with the cow.

We did a few more chores for her before it was time for us to leave.

*Not so bad,* Mrs. Falala said. *Tomorrow, you meet*

*Zora for official.*

*Zora? Who's Zora? Tomorrow? I'm not sure we can come back——*

*Yes, yes, your papa says eez fine. Three mornings a week.*

*But——*

*Watch out for Paulie——*

The squealing hog that we'd seen on our first visit came barreling around the side of the barn, chased once again by the fat, golden cat. We plastered ourselves against the barn and let them pass.

*Paulie is——the hog or the cat?*

*Paulie eez fat pig hog. Cat eez China. You come*

*back tomorrow. They'll be here. Zora, too.*

*Zora?*

*Zora eez cow.*

At the bottom of the drive, we stopped and stared back at the house, waiting to hear the flute music. It wasn't long, only a few minutes, before the gentle melody drifted out of the attic window.

## ZORA

(As I said, way back at the beginning . . . )

The truth is
Zora was ornery and stubborn
wouldn't listen to  a  n  y  b  o  d  y
and was selfish beyond selfish
and filthy
  caked with mud
     and dust
and moody:
you'd better watch it

**101**

or
she'd knock you
>           *f l a t*

>                    *s p l a t . . .*


That's Zora I'm talking about.
Zora
that
*cow.*


We found this out, me and Luke,
on our next visit to Mrs. Falala's.


*Bring her in,* commanded Mrs. Falala.


*Erm. How——*


*Get her. Bring her.*
Mrs. Falala tossed a halter in my direction.


**102**

*Come on, Lukey, we are going to do this.*

Surely I could imitate what I'd seen the kids do at the nearby Birchmere Farm. Surely I could just toss the loop over Zora's head and pull her on in. Right?

Lukey's eyes were open so wide. He stayed well behind me.

Zora was standing in a mud puddle when we approached her. When I tossed the loop at her head, she dodged it.

*Mooooo. Mooooooooo.*

*Talk to her, Reena. Tell her you're not going to hurt her.*

I talked to her. I told her I wouldn't hurt her.

I tossed the loop again.
She dodged it.
*Mooooo. Mooooooooo.*

Zora turned and walked farther away.
I tossed the rope from behind. Missed.
I tossed it again.
Zora stomped in the mud
        s    p    l    a    t    t    e    r    i    n    g
me from head
        to
            foot.

*Talk to her, Reena. Tell her not to be afraid.*
*Tell her——*

*Look, Luke, why don't YOU talk to her?*
*Why don't YOU try to get this halter on her?*

*Watch out, Reena——*

Zora had turned and was coming toward us.
She was picking up speed.

*Run, Luke—*

Zora was chasing us.
*Mooooooooo. Mooooooooo.*

When we reached the gate
Luke scrambled up and over it
instead of through it
and I was trying to follow
when Zora's
      E N O R M O U S   H E A D
loomed up below me and
               u   m  p
        b        e d
me into the air
so that I landed
ungracefully

on the other side
where
Mrs. Falala was standing
with a sly little smile on her
sly
little
face.

That Mrs. Falala!
That Zora!

*You didn't do it,* Mrs. Falala said, taking the halter from me and holding it aloft. *You think it eez too hard?*

We didn't answer.

*You babies?*

Luke stamped his foot. *We are* not *babies. Don't—*

**106**

*What Luke means is that we——we——*

*We are* not *babies!*

*Then do it,* said Mrs. Falala. *Put halter on Zora.* She dangled the rope in front of me.

You could practically see steam rising from Luke's head. He grabbed the rope, climbed the fence gate, and, sitting on the top rail, dropped the loop of the rope over Zora's big head while she stood perfectly still.

*There!* Luke said, tossing the loose end of the rope to Mrs. Falala. *There!*

*You catch flies with your open mouth,* Mrs. Falala said to me.

I couldn't have been more surprised if Luke had suddenly grown wings. He roped the cow?

**107**

That big-headed cow? And the cow didn't object?

Mrs. Falala opened the gate and handed the rope to me. *Bring Zora in.*

*To the stall?*

*Yes, yes, of course the stall. What you think, we are taking her to the grocery?*

There stood Zora. I gently tugged on the rope. *Come on, Zora, here we go.*

Nothing.

*Come on, time to eat.*

Zora moved backward, pulling hard. I dug in my heels, sliding in the muck.

*Come on, Zora.*

Luke said, *Tell her you won't hurt her. Tell her—*

I told her. I pulled. She pulled back.

*Tell her not to be afraid.*

I told her. Zora pulled. My heels slid in farther.
I fell on my butt.

That cow!

## MRS. FALALA'S PLAN

The next day, Mrs. Falala was waiting for us
at the barn.

*I tell you the plan, yes? You are not so good yet,
but you practice. You do all things and then you
will be ready.*

*Ready for what?* I asked.

Mrs. Falala opened the pasture gate and ushered
me and Luke inside. *Ready to show Zora.*

*What does that mean?*

She tossed me the rope. *Show her. At the fairs.*

*What fairs?*

Luke was standing there, swiveling his head from me to Mrs. Falala and back again, not saying a word.

*You don't know about fairs?* Mrs. Falala slapped her hand against her forehead. *Where you eez coming from that you don't know fairs?*

*You mean like a carnival?*

*Carnival? No! A fair. They show the horses, the cows, the pigs, the goats, the bunnies, the chickens. The judges choose best cow and best chicken and best piggy, like that. A fair. You got it now?*

Luke and I had never been to this sort of fair. In big cities, they don't show the horses, the cows, the pigs, the goats, the bunnies, or the chickens.

Mrs. Falala was waving us farther into the pasture. *Go. You get Zora. You think you can do it today?*

*I don't think Zora likes us,* I said.

*Of course not. She does not know you from nobody. What if you are bad person? You have to introduce yourself.*

On our way across the field, Luke practiced, *Hello, Zora. My name is Luke. This is Reena. We are not bad people.*

*I don't think she meant like that, Luke. I think she meant that Zora has to get used to us.*

Zora was not in the mood for introductions that day. She knocked me over with a push of her big, fat head, and she stubbornly refused to budge from her muddy spot near the bushes. She startled us frequently with loud *mooooo*s, she slobbered profusely, and then shook her head to splatter us with the slobber. She lifted her tail to let loose a long, smelly stream of urine and two runny dung pats. Flies zoomed around Zora and ventured over to us.

We returned to the barn without Zora.

Mrs. Falala clicked her tongue. *You might have to come more often.*

*But—but—* I tried to think of a polite protest but was caught off guard by Paulie the pig rounding the corner squealing. Paulie tore past me and knocked Luke flat, sending his notebook flying from his satchel.

Mrs. Falala retrieved the notebook. *What this eez?* She flipped through the pages.

*That's mine.*

*You make these pictures?*

*Yes.*

*You copy?*

*No.*

*How you do?*

Luke was looking up at Mrs. Falala, shielding his eyes from the sun. He staggered back, tugging at my arm. *Reena, Reena, up there—*

Slithering across the barn roof was the snake, long and thick and black.

Mrs. Falala followed our stares. *Eez just Edna.*
*She eats the mice.*

## A DAY OFF

We took a day off from going to Mrs. Falala's and rode our bikes all around the town. The sun was sparkling off the water and the boats in the harbor, and people were strolling along with their kids and their dogs and lined up at the ice cream stands and the lobster roll shack. We stopped at one stand for the creamiest soft-serve ice cream and got a cup of corn to feed the ducks in the river below. It was the perfect Maine-y kind of day.

Up Chestnut Street we rode and down the hill to the farm with the Belted Galloways, where we leaned our bikes against the fence. The girl and boy I'd seen before, Beat and Zep, waved from the barn.

*Where you been?* Beat called. *Haven't seen you in a few days.* She put down a bucket and walked up to where we were standing.

*Busy. Helping an old lady.*

*What old lady is that?* Beat was wearing the same orange overalls and tall black boots I'd seen her in before. She had sparkly black eyes and a kind smile.

*Mrs. Falala.*

Beat clapped her hand to her mouth. *Oh! Really? Mrs. Falala?*

*Yep. You know her?*

*Everyone knows Mrs. Falala.*

*Do you know her cow, Zora?*

Beat put her hand on my arm. *Oh boy, do I know Zora! Hey, Zep, come here. Look who's helping Mrs. Falala and zonky Zora.*

The tall, redheaded boy, Zep, ambled up to the fence. He nodded at me and at Luke. *That riot?*

*Pardon?* His Maine accent seemed stronger today.

He spoke louder, as if we were deaf.

*THAT RIGHT? YOU HELPING MRS. FALALA?*

*Erm. Yes.*

Beat and Zep exchanged a look that maybe meant *Are they crazy?* or maybe *Can you believe that?* or maybe *Poor kids.*

Beat said, *And they're helping her with Zora, too.*

*Whoa! Zora! Whoa! Now that's a stubborn one, that Zora.*

*Yes,* I said, *we discovered that. Mrs. Falala wants us to show Zora. At the fairs.*

Again, Beat and Zep exchanged a look.

*But,* I said, *we don't know anything about cows or fairs, do we, Luke?*

*Nope.*

Beat grinned. *Well, we can help you with that, can't we, Zep? We know about cows and we know about fairs, don't we, Zep?*

*Ayuh.*

So just like that, we arranged that Luke and I would come to the farm for a couple hours each of the days we did not go to Mrs. Falala's.

*We'll train you!* Beat said.

*Ayuh,* Zep agreed. *Train you riot up.*

## THE OUTFITS

One morning when we arrived at Mrs. Falala's, she said, *In barn, go see, now.* She flicked her hand at us, shooing us toward the barn.

There we found farm clothing intended for us: sturdy canvas overalls, long-sleeve denim shirts, tall black rubber boots, and thick suede work gloves.

*Eez not new,* Mrs. Falala said, as if to let us know she would never consider something so extravagant, *but eez good. Maybe a little big, but okay, eez good. Try. See.*

If, a few months ago, anyone had asked either me or Luke to wear these items, we would have refused. But now, Luke said, *Hey, just like Zep and Beat at the farm,* and I was thinking the same.

Mrs. Falala pulled on her braid. *Better to wear those when doing the work, yes? The work gets messy.*

Yes, we'd noticed that, and so had our parents, who said we were *extremely stinky* lately. They made us change in the garage before even coming inside and said our shoes were *foul.*

But now we had real farm gear.
It felt good.
But we tried not to show

*how* good
because we were a bit
*suspicious*
that Mrs. Falala had
done
something
nice
like
that.

She told us that we should leave the clothes
and boots in the barn at the end of each day.

*But maybe we could take them with us and bring
them back?* I asked.

*No.*

*We could use them at the farm—*

*What farm?*

Luke jumped in, rattling on about Beat and Zep and the Belties at Birchmere Farm, and then he pulled out his notebook and showed Mrs. Falala some of his drawings of the farm and the cows.

*Sit here,* she said. *Wait.* She made her way back to the house.

*Uh-oh,* I said. *Did we make her mad?*

*Were we dis-suspect—what's that word?*

*Disrespectful.*

*Were we that?* Luke asked.

Mrs. Falala emerged from the house carrying something pressed close to her chest. She sat on a hay bale beside Luke, and tapped on his notebook. *Show,* she commanded. *Show how!*

**124**

In her arms was a white tablet, which she placed on her lap. From a pocket she withdrew a stubby pencil. *Show!*

Maybe Mrs. Falala was not familiar with the word *please*. Mm?

*Show what?* Luke asked.

*That,* she said, tapping on Luke's open notebook. *How you do. Show to me.*

Luke cradled his notebook against his chest. *I don't—*

*You draw. Show to me.*

Mrs. Falala had pulled her braid around to the front and was chewing on the ends. She looked like a child sitting there on the hay bale, hair in her mouth, her small feet crossed one over the other. *Show how you do.*

Luke uncapped his black marker and turned to a fresh page. He looked around, his gaze settling on the open barn door. Quickly he sketched the outlines of the barn sides and roof and then the door frame. Mrs. Falala bent her head close, her eyes moving from his hands to the paper to the barn and back again.

Luke added a pig to the top of the barn and a fierce eagle swooping down on the pig.

*I no see that,* Mrs. Falala said.

Luke drew a braided dragon curling around the base of the barn.

*That not there,* Mrs. Falala said.

I opened the gate to the pasture and went in

126

search of Zora. She was not under her favorite bushes this time, but in the shadows of another corner of the pasture, near a small pond. Zora was facing me, standing completely still, the only movement the occasional swish of her tail. I approached her slowly, talking softly.

*It's just me. I'm Reena. Remember? I won't hurt you. It's okay.*

When I got within two feet of her, she spoke: *Moo. Mooooo.*

*Yes, yes,* I said. *Look, I don't even have a halter. I'm just here to see you.*

*Mooooo. Mooooo.*

I eased up beside her and carefully stroked her back. Her ears flicked this way and that.

*Mooooo.*

Zora was about four feet high and two feet wide and five feet long from end to end. At Birchmere, a heifer that Beat worked with weighed eight hundred pounds. Zora seemed only slightly smaller than that one.

Zora's fur was deep black on her face, neck, shoulders, and forefeet. Around her middle was a foot-wide belt of pure white fur, and behind was the deep black on her hindquarters, hind legs, and tail. I stroked her head and neck.

*Mooooo.*

I stroked her shoulders and back.

*Mooooo.*

I stood in front of her and looked into first

one big black eye and then the other. The eyes were so far apart, it was hard to look into both at the same time. Zora's nostrils were

(I believe I have mentioned)

ENORMOUS

and wet

and

d

r

i

p

p

y.

I stood there for some time, talking to her and stroking her head, and then I turned and walked away, saying, *See? I didn't want anything from you. I only came to visit.*

I was halfway back to the barn when I turned to look behind me, and there was Zora,

**following**

**me**

about ten feet behind, big head swinging from

          side        to        side.

I kept on walking, as if this was nothing
extraordinary
but inside
I was

# BURRR SSSTING !

Zora was

# F O L
#     L O W
#         I N G

    me.

I was hoping Mrs. Falala would notice, but her
head was still bent low over Luke's notebook,
watching him sketch. As I approached, she
pointed at Luke's drawing and said, *I no see this*

*or this or that.* She squinted at Luke. *Where this comes from?*

Luke offered his marker to Mrs. Falala. *You try.*

She clapped her hands to her chest. *No, no—*

*Didn't you ever draw before?*

Mrs. Falala sat up straight. *No. I do not draw.*

*Never?*

*Never.*

I couldn't imagine that. Never? How could a person live a whole life and never draw? Not a tree or a house or a stick figure or a cat or a dog or a flower? Nothing? Never?

*Mooooo. Mooooooooo.*

Zora was pressed up against the fence, her BIG nostrils poking between the slats.

*Well, well,* Mrs. Falala said. *Now you have new friend?*

# SETBACK

After spending a morning over at Birchmere Farm where Beat and Zep let us help as they trained and groomed their cows, we returned to Mrs. Falala's, eager to practice what we'd learned.

No sign of Mrs. Falala when we arrived, but Paulie the pig was snorting in a mud hole behind the barn and the parrot was squawking from the barn roof. The fat cat stood watch over a bush, its head darting left and right, tracking something. No sign of the snake.

Zora was standing in the shade beside her favorite bush on the far side of the pasture. I wondered if Zora got tired standing around all day. Was she bored? Was she lonely? What did she think about?

*Hey, Zora!* I called. *I'm back! Did you miss me?*

We climbed the fence rails and dropped to the other side and crossed the pasture.

It wasn't until we were within five feet of her that she suddenly let out a
# loud
## bellowing
### *Moooooooooo*
startling us so that we stopped in our tracks.

*Zora?*

Another
## loud
### belligerent
### bellowing
*Moooooooooo*

and with that she turned around and butted Luke with her enormous head and knocked him to the ground. She then butted her head at me, knocking me backward.

*Mooooooooo. Mooooooooo.*

She swung that big head from side to side, turned her back to us, and moved off.

We tried once more to approach her, but she whipped her head around, swished her tail like a whip, butted me in the stomach, and bellowed angrily.

*Mooooo, mooooooooo*
*Mooooo, mooooooooo.*

Luke had attached himself to my arm. *Come on, Reena, let's go back to the barn. Please, Reena? Please?*

We stepped slowly away from Zora, backtracking across the pasture, keeping our eyes on her the whole way.

When we reached the barn, Mrs. Falala was standing in the open doorway.

*So,* she said, *how's your little Zora friend today, mm? Not so friendly?*

## MUCKING ABOUT

I was mucking out Zora's stall
scooping up manure patties
and
    d
        u
            m
                p
                    i
                        n
                          g

them in the wheelbarrow.

Luke and Mrs. Falala were sitting
              side          by          side
on a hay bale
with their notebooks open.


When Luke drew, his small hand moved
                  *fast*
his pen gliding across the white paper.


When Mrs. Falala drew, her gnarly hand
crept along
        s     l     o     w     l     y
so very very
        s     l     o     w     l     y.


For three days she had been drawing
                  the head of a cow—
at least that is what I thought she was drawing
but there was not enough of it to be sure.


Luke's lines flowed smoothly.

There was movement in the figures.

Mrs. Falala's lines were stiff.
Maybe the cow was dead.

## COLOR

Along the roads
the lupines grew
tall spears of color
pink and white and blue
and beyond lay vast carpets
of buttercups
and up and down the roads
we rode our bikes.

*Hello, lupines,*
*hello, buttercups,*
*hellooooo, Maine,*
*we love you.*

## BUGS

What were these tiny black things
that flew into your eyes and ears
and slipped up your sleeves and
down your socks
and
     BIT
you?

They were not mosquitoes
they were barely visible
but when the day was still

when the wind was calm

these tiny black bugs

sssssswwwwwwwwaaaaaaarrrrrrrmmmmmed

and bit

and then you

ITCHITCHITCHITCHED!!!

We were covered with red welts

and we

SCRAAAAAAAATCHED

all

day

long.

## BODILY FLUIDS

One day I succeeded in haltering Zora and was trying to comb her with the sturdy metal comb that Mrs. Falala had shoved into my hands when we arrived. I thought Zora might like the feel of the comb through her fur, and for a few minutes it seemed that she did.

And then I hit a snag,
a tangled, matted knot of hair
and pulled hard and

that big head swung toward me
and knocked against my arm
scolding me
as a wide swath of mucus
dripped out of her nose
and down my sleeve.

Her wet slobbery tongue
slapped against my wrist.

She lifted her tail
unleashing a wide, steamy stream
of
urine
        *s p*
            *la   sh*
                    *i  n  g*
my pants and boots.

*Oh, that's good!* Luke called from the fence.

*I'm gonna draw* that!

About that time, along came Paulie the pig. He dashed toward and beneath Zora, who kicked at him, and, missing him, Zora got me instead.

*That pig! What good is that pig?* I yelled.

Mrs. Falala poked her head out of the barn door and said, *Paulie eez part of family. What if someone ask your mama what good are* you?

## LONELY

On my bike
riding to Mrs. Falala's
Luke ahead of me
bobbing his head
and singing a song
he made up as he pedaled:

> *Gonna ride, ride,*
> *gonna fly, fly,*
> *gonna zip, zip . . .*

And I felt lucky
that Luke was with me
that I wasn't wandering
this new town
alone.

We pulled into Mrs. Falala's drive
stashed our bikes
put on our work clothes
and found Zora
still in her stall
standing against the rail
her head hanging low
and
something popped in my chest
sending bubbles floating up to my brain.

*Luke,* I said, *Zora is* lonely.

*Aw,* Luke said.
*Aw, poor Zora.*

**148**

I entered the stall
and approached Zora slowly.
Gently I stroked her neck.

*You're lonely, aren't you, girl?*

Zora moved her head
toward me.
She rested her head against
my arm.

That day I told Mrs. Falala
that Zora was lonely
that Zora needed company
that she must be very sad
to be all alone.

Mrs. Falala mashed her lips
together and said,
*Zora eez not alone.*
*I am here.*

*Paulie the pig eez here.*
*So eez Cat, so eez Parrot,*
*so eez Edna Snake.*

I said,
*But there are no other cows.*
*No one for her to lean against.*
*No one for her to talk to.*

Mrs. Falala said nothing.
She turned around and
walked back to the house
that long white braid
swinging slowly
left to right
right to left.

# FOG

Down to the harbor
early one Saturday morning
Mom and Dad and me and Luke
before
         the tourists swarmed
before
         the stores opened.

Soft, gray
         *fffffffog*
         hovered

over the water
masking the moored boats.

We climbed down to the small
stretch of beach
seaweed and mussel shells
splayed across the rocks.

Fish smell and salt air
mast creaks and rope jangles.

And as we stood there
the fog rose
slowly, surely,
revealing first the hulls
and then the masts
of wooden vessels
their sails
rolled
into

      cocoons
and lobster boats wave-rolling
and red-blue-yellow buoys bobbing.

My mother said,
*Oh!*
*Did you ever see anything*
*like that*
*ever*
*in your life?*

And I was thinking that
I never saw anything like
*everything* I was seeing
never saw anything like
those everythings
ever
in
my
life.

Sometimes I had to
close my eyes
to rest them from
all the new everythings
pouring in.

## DREAMS

At night I dreamed of Zora
of her wide furry body
and her giant head
and her huge black eyes

and in the dreams
I combed her
and talked with her
and she was warm
and comforting

and I smelled the sawdust
in her stall
and felt the softness of her fur
and in the dream
she talked to me.

She said
*Yes, I am lonely.*
*Yes, I am.*

So I stroked her
and combed her
and told her
that I would find
some company
for her.

## PLANS

I was nervous, nervous, but I geared up my courage and talked first to Beat and Zep and then to the owners of Birchmere Farm. I was afraid they would laugh at me, but they didn't.

*Of course,* they said. *She needs to be around other cows. Of course.*

They said that I could bring Zora to their farm where there was plenty of room and plenty of other cows, as long as I took care of her.

*Zora comes from a long line of Grand Champions,*
Mr. Birch said. *Did you know that?*

No, I did not.

*And she should show well as long as you can keep
that temper of hers under control.*

Beat and Zep would help me train Zora and
they would train me, too, so that I would
know how to show Zora at the fair.

*A long line of Grand Champions!*

That sounded impressive, didn't it? It sounded
like a perfect plan, right?

## A LONG LINE

Mrs. Falala was not so excited about the plan.

*Move Zora? Take my Zora? That eez not happening.*

*But she would have company,* I said. *Lots and lots of company.*

Mrs. Falala waved my words away with one hand.

I *am the company of Zora,* Mrs. Falala said. *Me*

*and Edna and Paulie and China and Crockett. We are plenty company.*

Mrs. Falala sat on the hay bale that had become her regular seat for drawing with Luke. Patting the bale next to her, she opened her notebook and looked up at Luke expectantly.

*But,* I persisted, *look how sad Zora seems. Look how she hangs her head. Listen to those sad moos.*

*That eez not sad hanging head!* Mrs. Falala snapped. *Those are not sad moos. Those are normal cow moos and normal cow heads.*

I said, *I hear Zora comes from a long line of Grand Champions.*

Mrs. Falala clicked her tongue and tapped her pencil on her notebook. *You want to see Grand Champions?* she said. *Go look in barn, past the*

*halters, go on, you go look,*
*Luke and I have drawing to do.*

Along a wooden rail
at one end of the barn
near the halters and ropes
and rakes and shovels
and buckets and barrels
hung a row of photos
the images clouded over
with dust and cobwebs.

With a rag, I cleared away the glass.
In each was a Beltie
and a young woman
holding a medallion and blue ribbon:
### *Grand Champion.*

I looked closely at the women and wondered if
maybe they were all the same person, growing
older.

I returned to Mrs. Falala and Luke, their heads bent over their notebooks.

*That's you, isn't it?* I said. *In those photographs with the Grand Champions—that's you.*

Mrs. Falala said, *I lie down now.* Abruptly, she stood and returned to the house, calling behind her, *Don't take my Zora.*

## A FRIEND

When Beat and Zep heard about Mrs. Falala's refusal to move Zora to Birchmere Farm, Zep offered to bring one of his own heifers to Mrs. Falala's.

*To keep Zora company,* Zep said, *to be an example for Zora.*

Beat chimed in, *Oh, yes! You should send Yolanda, definitely Yolanda.*

Yolanda was smaller than Zora, quiet and sweet. She didn't bump us or slobber on us or whack her tail at us.

We were excited to tell Mrs. Falala about this offer, so excited that we didn't wait until the next morning. We found Mrs. Falala walking up her drive, trailed by China, the golden fat cat. We told her the news—that Zep had offered to bring Yolanda over to keep Zora company.

Luke was clapping his hands to try to contain his excitement.

But Mrs. Falala was not excited. She carried on walking. *I am telling you that Zora already has company and besides who would take care of that extra animal? You think I want that extra work? And who would pay for the grain?*

Luke and I stopped. We turned our bikes around.

And then we heard a loud
> *Mooooo*

and then more
> *Mooooo, mooooo, mooooooooo.*

Luke said, *Zora is calling us, Reena. We can't just leave without saying hello.*

We left our bikes and walked up to the barn where we found Zora nudging her huge nose against a rail.
> *Mooooo. Mooooo.*

It was a friendly sound that day, and when we reached her, she leaned her head against my arm.

Luke patted her side. *There, there,* he whispered. *Don't be lonely, Zora. We are here.*

Mrs. Falala came up behind us. *Okay, okay, okay,* she said. *The friend cow can come but only for a visit, only a week or two, and you have to take care of it. Are you hearing me?*

*Yes, yes! We are hearing you!*

We stayed longer and cleaned out the bay
and refilled the grain bin
and led Zora around the pasture
and hosed her off
and combed her hair
and told her about
the new cow friend
     **Yo   land   a**
who would come the next day.

As we were leaving, Mrs. Falala
clicked her tongue and said,
*Paulie will be jealous.*

*The pig?* Luke said.
*Why would Paulie be jealous?*

*Because he'll want a friend, too,*
Mrs. Falala said.
She turned her back on us
and swung that long braid
left and right
and disappeared into her house.

## YOLANDA ARRIVES

Zep and Beat and Mr. Birch from the farm brought Yolanda in the truck to Mrs. Falala's. Yolanda was all cleaned up for the occasion: her fur shiny and smooth, her hooves clean, and her head and neck boasting a new green bridle.

Zep led her to the outdoor pen where Zora was standing, munching on a bit of hay. Both Zora and Yolanda lifted their heads but did not make a sound.

Zora flicked her tail.
Yolanda flicked her tail.

We stood by the fence watching, me and
Luke and Zep and Beat. I looked back toward
the house and saw Mrs. Falala at the kitchen
window, but she quickly ducked out of the way.

Zora seemed confused. Her head moved
slowly, taking in
  *Yo land a*
and all of us at the fence. She backed up.

I was so nervous. I feared Zora would kick
Yolanda or bellow at her or butt her with her
big head.

The two of them
stood there
and
stood there

and
stood there
and
stood there.

*Urggggg!*

It was so frustrating
so nerve-wracking
the watching
and waiting.

A mud ball emerged
from around the back of the barn:
Paulie the pig
snorting and snuffling
covered with mud.

He squeezed under
the bottom rail of the fence
and into the pen

and straight over to Yolanda
snorting and snuffling
and sniffing
while
Yolanda stood perfectly still

and then China the cat
her back arched
her fur on end
zoomed into view
and under the rail
circling Yolanda
while
Yolanda stood perfectly still

and then
Crockett the parrot
flapped and squawked
up and over the fence
and onto Yolanda's back
while

Yolanda stood perfectly still.

And at last Zora moved.
She approached Yolanda.
She nudged Paulie and China away
and she batted her head at Crockett
sending the parrot flying off.

Zora sidled up to Yolanda
and the two stood there
side by side
making no sound.

They just
stood there
and
stood there
and
stood there.

# TRAINING

For an hour each day, Zep joined us at Mrs. Falala's to work with Yolanda and to show me how to train Zora for two events at the upcoming fair. One event would judge the cows and one would judge the people showing the cows. I asked Zep if the judging was done in front of an audience.

Zep leaned his forehead close to mine. He said, *Well, you're not going to show Zora in a closet. You afraid of an audience?*

*No, I am not. I just have no idea what to expect.*

*You don't think you can handle it?*

*I can handle it, Zep.* And even if I couldn't, I wasn't going to admit it to him.

*You'll have to work really hard to get Zora ready and to learn what to do——*

*——I can work hard——*

*——and I'll help you.*

My mouth flopped open like a thirsty dog.

Zep smiled his slow, full smile and turned his head to one side.

I was embarrassed down to the tips of my boots. I wanted to be able to train Zora right

**174**

and show her well, and I needed his help.

We practiced out in the pasture, the heifers tethered to us by their halters.

*Heads up,* Zep said, *you* and *Zora. Back straight. Follow me. Watch.*

Zora was not cooperative. I tugged. I pulled. Three steps forward. Stop. Tug. Pull. Five steps. She was being stubborn and ornery. Meanwhile, Zep and Yolanda moved on smoothly, walking a wide circle with no stopping and no tugging.

Luke and Mrs. Falala were sitting on the hay bales drawing. From time to time they glanced up at us and then back to their paper.

Zora moved forward and, mid-stride, dropped a ***plop*** of manure.

*What if she does that in the show?*

*They* all *do it,* Zep said. *It's natural.*

*But everybody's walking round and round and stepping in it?*

*Nah, there'll be pickers there. They scoop it up.*

Well, then: manure plops and pickers and scooping. It was natural, right?

The training was harder than I expected. Most days it was hot and dusty, and after coaxing Zora to let me halter her and lead her around, my arms and legs were weak with fatigue. Then I still had to tend to her food and water and clean out her pen. But the surprising thing to me was that I *liked* doing it. I liked the hard work. I liked seeing Zora respond a little more each day, and I liked feeling stronger.

Luke helped me with cleaning out the pen and brushing Zora, and I could tell that he liked it, too. He wanted to be in charge of cleaning out the buckets and hanging up the brushes and halters. He talked to Zora and Yolanda all the time, letting them know that they were good cows. *Not lumpy at all,* he told them.

Luke was less afraid of Mrs. Falala now, too. He wasn't flinching when she sat beside him on the hay bales, and she wasn't barking so many orders at us. Often, I saw her and Luke talking while they drew, side by side.

Little changes, day by day.

## RAIN DAY

One day as Luke and I were halfway to Mrs. Falala's
the rain began

|   |   |
|---|---|
| p | d |
| o | o |
| u | w |
| r | n |
| i |   |
| n |   |
| g |   |

in straight torrents from the skies

drenching us
our shirts plastered to our skin
our hair flattened on our heads.

We raced to the barn
just as lightning
    **cracked**
and
    **FLASHED**
and thunder
    **boooooooooomed**
and
    rumbled
overhead.

We cowered in the stall beside Zora and Yolanda
who were lying side by side in the sawdust.
It smelled of cows and rain and piney chips
and their fur was warm and soft
as we leaned against them.
And I thought I could stay all day

right there
cradled
by
cows.

## SAD ZEP

Zep arrived one morning looking limp—
as if someone had let the air out of his body
no trace of a smile
sad, sad, droopy mouth
eyes swollen and red.

He went quickly to Yolanda and Zora
and rubbed his hand across their heads
and sides
and looked into their eyes
and touched their wet noses

and turned to us and said
that one of the cows at Birchmere
had died
in the night.

He found her lying on her side
in her stall
her head against the wall
her legs tucked daintily beneath her.

*Died?* Luke said.
*Died? How could a cow die?*

Zep blinked
once    twice    three    times.

*Well, this one, she caught something—*
*something respiratory probably.*
*We're not sure yet.*

*You mean like pneumonia?*

**182**

*A cow can get that?*

*Yes, something like that.*

Both Luke and I patted Zora.
*But Zora's okay, right?*
*And Yolanda, right?*

Luke stared into Zora's big black eyes.
*Cows shouldn't die.*

Zep put his hand on Luke's shoulder.
Zep opened his mouth, closed it
opened it again.

*The cows at the farm—*
Zep said—
*some we keep for breeding,*
*and some for showing, sure,*
*but you know where the rest go, right?*

Luke and I shared one last moment of
mutual innocence.

*No. Where?* Luke said.

Zep looked up at the barn rafters
and then down at the straw on the floor
and then he scratched behind one ear
and finally he said,
*Hamburger.*

## WHAAAAT?


How did we not know this?
What did we think that whole field of cows
at the farm was going to do?
Keep on happily munching grass
in the rolling green field
for all the days of their lives?

And Zora?
And Yolanda?
Were they going to become—

I
can't
say
it—
urkkkkkk
*h a m b u r g e r ????*

*Noooooooooo.*

## SYMPATHY?

At home that night, we had soup for dinner.
Luke eyed his suspiciously.

*What kind of soup is this?*

My mother said, *chicken noodle, you know that.*

*Is there any hamburger in it?*

*Noooo,* my mother said. *Just chicken and noodles
and carrots and celery, like always.*

*Do you* want *hamburger in your chicken noodle soup?*

Luke clapped his hands to his cheeks. *No, no, no. No more hamburger.*

My father tapped Luke on the head. *What's up with you tonight? What's with the sudden aversion to hamburger?*

*The cows!* Luke said. *The poor, innocent cows!*

*Ahh. The cows,* Dad said.

I felt queasy. *Let's be vegetarians,* I said.

My parents considered this, nodding, studying the ceiling.

*So, no more steaks?* my father said, wincing painfully.

**188**

*Or pot roast?* my mother said. *Or chili? Or tacos?*

In a very small voice, Luke said, *But I really like tacos.*

My mother halted her spoon on its route to her mouth. *Vegetarian? What about this soup then?*

*What about it?* asked Luke.

*It's chicken noodle.* Chicken *noodle.*

Luke's spoon clattered into his bowl. *From chickens? You mean like* real *ones?*

I pushed my bowl away. Luke did the same.

My dad said, *And then there's bacon. You love bacon, Reena.*

Uh-oh.

*What's wrong with bacon?* Luke asked.

Dad said, *You know where bacon comes from.*

Luke thought.
His face contorted.
The horror!
*Pigs!* he said.
*Paulie!*
*Poor, innocent Paulie!*

My parents looked at each other.
*Paulie?* they said.
*Who's that?*

## AGITATION

The next day at Mrs. Falala's
Luke and I were
        a g i t a t e d
bombarding her with
        Q Q Q Q Questions Q Q Q Q
about Zora.

*What will happen to her?*
*Will she die?*
*Are you going to eat her?*

Mrs. Falala smiled wickedly.
*Yes,* she said, *I am going to*
              *CHOP*
*her up and make a*
              *ZILLION*
       *HAMBURGERS . . .*

but she stopped talking
when she saw Luke crying—
his fists against his eyeballs
his shoulders heaving
tears
running
down
his
face.

She took Luke's hand.
*No,* she whispered.
*I am not going to chop up Zora*
*and eat her.*

**192**

*I am not going to turn her into*
*hamburger.*
*I was kidding.*
*Really.*
*Really.*

Luke tapped his chin.
*What about Paulie?*
*Are you going to eat Paulie?*

*Oh,* Mrs. Falala said.
*Well, now.*
*He would make such very good*
    *BACON . . .*
*No, no, no, don't cry!*
*I don't mean it!*
*I'm not going to eat Paulie.*

*Promise?*

*Promise.*

## FACE THE FACTS

Once we were satisfied that Mrs. Falala was not going to eat Zora and that Zora would be saved for breeding more Belted Galloways, and once we understood that Paulie was a pet—a runt pig to whom Mrs. Falala had become attached—we calmed down.

And then Zep arrived and we started in on him: *What will happen to Yolanda? Will she die? Will she become hamburger? What about the other cows at the farm?*

In Zep's slow-moving, slow-talking way, he explained that Yolanda, like Zora, would be used for breeding more Belted Galloways, but that the calves born *without* the white belt of fur around their middles would be sold for beef and most of the steers (the males) would as well.

*People eat meat, Zep said. Face the facts. It's a hard thing to adjust to, I realize. But I'm going to be a farmer and raise the best beef cows in Maine. I love cows, and I'm going to treat them good as long as I can.*

Luke walked the length of the barn
and lay down on a hay bale
and stared up at the sky.

He didn't say anything.
He just lay there
looking up at that sky.

And when I was done with chores
I joined him
and the two of us
lay still
looking up at that sky.

# SHOW STICK

One day Mrs. Falala handed me

             a

             long

             thin

             lightweight

             metal

             rod

             with

             a

             short

             L-shaped

molded

hook

at     one     end.

*Eez show stick,* she said. *You need for fair.*
*Watch.*

Usually it was Zep who worked with me and
Zora, teaching me how to lead her in the ring,
my back straight, eyes on the judge, attentive
and calm, gently keeping Zora by my side, one
hand firmly gripping the halter.

But on that day, Mrs. Falala held up the show
stick and said, *Watch.*

She stood in front of Zora and with the hook
end of the pole, she gently stroked Zora's chest
and on up her neck, rhythmically and slowly,
up and down, down and up.

*You see how calm eez Zora?*

Zora stood perfectly still, lazily blinking, calm, calm. Mrs. Falala moved to Zora's side and with the show stick, she tapped one of Zora's hind legs, urging it back a few inches. She reached behind the other leg and coaxed it forward slightly.

*See? Good stance. All gentle. See?*

Mrs. Falala ran the show stick beneath Zora's belly, back and forth, forth and back, softly, gently.

*See? Calm.*

When Zep arrived, Mrs. Falala handed me the show stick and said, *Practice.* She headed for the barn, her long braid swinging, and there

was Zora
her tail swishing

                left to right
                right to left

the braid
and
the tail
      swish
            swish
      swish
            swish.

## BEAUTY DAY

Animals needed *primping* for the fair:
    shampoos
    clipping
    pedicures (hoof-i-cures?)

I am not kidding!

Zep declared **Beauty Day** for Zora and
Yolanda.
    We lathered

we scrubbed
we rinsed
we dried them with a blow-dryer.

I am not kidding!

We clipped
we combed
we brushed.
We cleaned and polished hooves.

*You'll have to do it all again at the fair,*
Zep said.
*This is just round one: preparation.*

It made us laugh.
Beauty Day for the heifers!
They looked SO good when we were done!

And then Zora tromped through

a mud puddle
and lay down
and said
     *Moo.*

## TO THE FAIR

At five a.m. on the day of the fair, Dad and Mom drove us to Mrs. Falala's. We were haltering Zora and Yolanda when Zep and Mr. Birch from Birchmere Farm arrived with a cattle van. Inside were six other cows haltered to the rail, blinking lazily.

Zep led Yolanda up the ramp and into the van and returned for Zora, who balked.

*Talk to her,* Zep said to me. *Tell her it's okay.*

Leaning in close, I stroked her head and whispered, *Zora, girl, we are going to the fair. All of us. I'll be there with you.*

*Moooooo.*

I took the halter from Zep and tugged at it, and eventually, after a little more snorting and stomping and swinging her head, Zora followed me up the ramp and settled in beside Yolanda.

My parents looked at me as if I'd just done a triple flip in the air.

Zep and Mr. Birch locked up the ramp and we returned to our own car, ready to follow them up to the fair, about an hour away.

*Wait!* I said. *Where is Mrs. Falala?* I realized we hadn't seen her yet that morning. *Isn't she coming?*

We all turned toward the house. No lights on, all dark, all quiet.

*She's probably still sleeping,* Dad said, *like most people at this hour. Let her sleep.*

As our car turned to follow the van pulling out of the drive, I noticed that the attic window was open, but I heard no music, no flute.

On the way to the fair, Luke said, *Did anyone actually* ask *Mrs. Falala if she wanted to go to the fair?*

I hadn't even thought about it. *I just assumed she was going,* I said.

*Wouldn't she want to see Zora in the ring?* Luke asked.

*I guess not.*

**206**

# FAIRGROUNDS

Rows of cattle vans
   people swarming, old and young
      cotton candy! fried dough! fudge!
      hot dogs! tacos! doughnuts!
   beef cattle and dairy cows
     sheep and chickens
         pigs and rabbits
moos and baas
   oinks and neighs

flowers and crafts
show rings and bleachers
games and rides

Ferris Wheel! Bumper Cars!

Such a world of its own
this fairsweet fairswarm
haven.

## MORE PRIMPING

Rows of cows being groomed:
    sudsing, fluffing, drying,
    combing, spraying, polishing.

A loudspeaker crackled:
*Thirty minutes, Group One!*

Along the rows the older teens
quickened their pace.
Zep and Beat tucked in their shirts
wiped off their boots

slipped cow combs in their back pockets
grabbed their show sticks
did a final once-over of their heifers
          Yolanda and YoYo
and off they marched into the ring.

Instead of sitting in the bleachers, we stood by the arena rail with Mr. Birch, who explained what was happening. This part was for show-manship: the judges were studying both the animals and their handlers, but final judging in this round centered on the handlers. How well were they showing their animals?

The teens led their animals clockwise around the ring, and then reversed. The judge lined them up, parallel to each other, and walked back and forth, pausing to study the setup of this or that animal, and pausing to question the handlers.

We overheard some of the questions: *How much does she weigh? When was she born?*

I panicked. What if I were asked these questions about Zora? I didn't know the answers. Sensing my agitation, Mr. Birch reminded me that Zora was a fall heifer and now weighed about eight hundred pounds.

The judge moved over to Beat, who stood tall and confident by her heifer, YoYo, and then along the line and finally to Zep and Yolanda.

I had been watching Zep closely, the way he used the show stick to calm Yolanda, the way he adjusted Yolanda's stance, moving one foot slightly back, the other slightly forward, all while keeping his attention on the judge. He was so at ease and so gentle with Yolanda, and so at ease with the judge, who, after asking

Zep several questions, nodded appreciatively
before moving on.

The judge walked up and down the line one
more time, studying, until at last he called
out the first and second place showmanship
winners. We didn't know them.

Third place showmanship went to
　　　　oh yes
　　　　　　it did
　　　　　　　　it went
　　　　　　　　　to
　　　　　　　　　　that redheaded boy
　　　　　　　　　　　with the long legs:
　　　　　　　　　　　*Zep.*

He nodded at the judge.
He nodded at me.

# SHOWTIME!

Oh, that Zora!
She let me halter her
and lead her to the ring
so perfectly obedient
and calm.

She stood there with me
as we waited in line
with eleven other novices
and their heifers or steers.

She let me stroke her neck
with the show stick
and she let me comb
the hair along her back.

When our group was announced
the entrants in front of us
moved forward.

*Okay, okay, I can do this.*
*Just walk,* I told myself.
*Stand straight.*
*Smile.*

I was excited.
I loved everything about it:
the ring, the sawdust,
the cows, the handlers,
the men and women and kids
on the bleachers and along the fence.

I was looking for Zep.
I wanted him to see how well I was doing.
I wanted him to see how I held the show stick
and how straight my back was
and how calm I was and
how loosely I could hold the halter.

We were near the entry gate.
Zora looked into the ring
and snorted
and then she

## BOLTED.

## CATCH THAT HEIFER

Zora had yanked the halter from my
carelessly loose grip
and took off
kicking and bucking
>    *Moooooo*
>    *Moooooo*

I chased her as she ran past the stalls
knocking over buckets
and brooms and rakes
>    *Moooooo*

216

*Moooooo*

People dodged out of her way
calling
> *Cow on the loose!*
> *Cow on the loose!*

Beat and Zep and Mr. Birch
joined in the chase
> *Cow on the loose!*
> *Cow on the loose!*

*Moooooo*
*Moooooo*

Who knew a cow could run so fast?

I turned back once to look at the ring:
the novices and the judge
and my parents and Luke
all stood there

staring
at
the
  *cow on the loose*

and the chaos erupting
around and behind
that
wild-eyed
heifer:
Zora.

## SHOWMANSHIP

Zora raced down the chicken aisle
and careened past the rabbit cages,
nearly landing amid a pen of squealing piglets.

People leaped out of the way.

Zep and I finally caught her
and led her back to the stalls
where she snatched a clomp of hay
and chewed defiantly
and slurped water from the hose

as if nothing whatever was wrong.

The novice showmanship competition
was
over.

We had missed it.

## BREED

Next up was the breed round.

*What do you think?* Zep asked me.
*Willing to try Zora again for the breed event?*

My parents and Luke joined us.
Luke moved up close to Zora
and placed his small hand on her wide neck.
*Zora, you be good. You know how.*

Mom and Dad looked surprised.

*We had no idea you could do all this, Reena.*


I had a quick glimpse of me in my room
in our old apartment back in the city
*an inside girl*
and now here I was
*an outside girl*
*a*
*cow*
*girl.*


When the Belted Galloway breed was called
I led Zora back to the ring
and we entered
like civilized partners
and circled the ring
without too much contrariness
and she let me calm her with the show stick
and she did not drop any plops of anything
and she did not kick anyone or anything.


222

As the judge moved along the row asking
questions
I kept stroking Zora with the show stick
praying that she would stay calm
praying that she would not bolt.

When the judge reached us, he said,
*You're new at this?*

*Yes.*

*Are you nervous?*

*Yes.*

*Well, you don't show it. That's good.
And you did a fine job regaining control
of your animal earlier. I saw that.
What's her name?*

*Zora.*

*And when was she born?*

*Fall of last year.*

*And how much does she weigh?*

*Eight hundred pounds.*

*And who were her parents?*

*Her . . . parents?*

*Yes, what's her lineage?*

*Her . . . lineage? I'm sorry, sir,*
*but I do not know.*

*Well, you surprise me.*
*This looks like a fine young heifer*
*and I would think you'd want to know*
*what her lineage is.*

**224**

*My guess is that there's a champion*
*in there somewhere.*

*Oh! Yes, wait. I think that's right.*
*I think she comes from*
 *a long line of champions.*

*You* think?

*I'm new at this. I'm sorry.*

*Don't worry, next time you'll know,*
*won't you?*

*Yes, sir.*

Zora placed fourth out of nine
and received praise from the judge
for her fine proportions
and good lines.

*And you,* he said to me,
*have good posture and a nice smile*
*and a good relationship with Zora.*

*But——she bolted earlier——*

The judge patted Zora's back.
*Oh, just a little stubbornness.*
*The important thing is*
*you didn't lose your cool*
*and you tried again.*

As we left the ring, I stroked Zora's head
and whispered to her
*Do you hear that?*
*We have a good relationship.*

I was eager to see Zep and my family,
and as I searched the crowd for them,
I spotted a woman with a long, white braid

but
it was not
Mrs. Falala.

I felt sorry that she wasn't there
but then I told myself
maybe she would have been
disappointed.
In Zora.
In me.

But there were others who were
not disappointed.

My parents' smiles were so wide
and my mom kept saying
*How do you do that?*
*How did you learn all that?*

Luke ran up to me and hugged my waist

and would not let go.
*It was so good, Reena. Wasn't it good?*
*Was it fun? Did you like it?*

Zep followed me
as I returned to the stall with Zora.
He leaned in close to her
and stroked her head
and looked her in the eyes
and said
*You were riot good, Zora.*
*Riot good.*

He turned to me and leaned in close
and said
*You, too, Reena.*
*You were riot good.*

## RIDES

After all the Beltie events, Zora was loaded
in the van with Yolanda and with the other
animals from Birchmere Farm. Zep promised
to resettle Zora and Yolanda back at Mrs.
Falala's, so Mom, Dad, Luke, and I stayed on
at the fair.

Luke wanted me to go on all the rides with
him, and even though I felt too old for that,
I went because Luke begged and because I
secretly wanted to go on them anyway.

Roller coaster! Tilt-A-Whirl! Even my parents joined us on the Ferris wheel. We were all laughing and loving the fair and it felt only right to also eat cotton candy and hot dogs. That's what you do at the fair, right?

It was nearly seven o'clock when we left.

On the ride home, I thought about Zora and how well she'd done—once she got over her first bolting escapade—and I wanted to tell Mrs. Falala that. I asked my parents if we could stop there on the way, but just before we pulled in her drive, I changed my mind.

*What if she ruins it?* I said.

Mom turned to look at me. *What do you mean, Reena?*

*Well, it's been such a good day. What if Mrs. Falala*

*isn't happy about something?*

*Like what?*

*I don't know—like maybe that Zora bolted the first time and then only came in fourth in the breed event.*

Luke had been quiet on the ride home, drawing in his notebook, but now he said, *It was the best day ever, and you and Zora did the best job ever, and I will tell Mrs. Falala that if she says anything mean.*

I love that Lukey boy.

Dad said, *Well, let's take a vote. How many think we should go knock on her door and maybe wake her up and get her mad?*

Silence.

*Okay, then, how many think we should go on home
and wait to see Mrs. Falala tomorrow?*

The vote was unanimous. We went on home.

## PHONE CALL

Early the next morning, my parents received
a phone call from someone named Mr. Colley.
He asked if they could meet him at Mrs.
Falala's house.

My dad was hardly awake when he answered
the phone, so he agreed without even asking
why.

Luke said, *Uh-oh, you're in trouble now, Reena.*

233

*Me, why me, Luke? Maybe you're the one in trouble?*

*I don't think so. You're the one who took her cow to the fair.*

Dad wanted to know if we'd been disrespectful again. Mom asked if we knew who Mr. Colley was.

*And oh,* Dad said, *Mr. Colley said that you and Luke should stay home. 'It would be best,' Mr. Colley said.*

## SPECULATION

While Mom and Dad were gone, Luke and I
tried to imagine all the possible reasons that
they had been summoned to Mrs. Falala's and
who Mr. Colley was.

*He could be anybody!*
*A policeman, a fireman, a plumber*
*a doctor, repairman, or vet*
*a lawyer, a salesman,*
*a relative, a friend.*

*Maybe Mrs. Falala's house burned down.*
*Maybe something happened to Zora.*

*No, no, no, don't say that.*
*Don't even think those bad things.*

*When will Mom and Dad be home?*
*What's taking them so long?*

*What if we're in trouble?*
*Did we disrespect?*
*Is Mrs. Falala mad at us?*
*Does she want us never to come back?*

*Maybe she had a heart attack.*
*Maybe she fell down and broke her bones.*
*Maybe she has pneumonia.*
*Maybe she's in the hospital.*

*No, no, no, don't say those bad things.*
*Don't think them.*

**236**

*When will Mom and Dad be home?*
*What is taking*
*so*
*so*
*long*gggggggggggggggggg?

## WAITING

Time time time
someTIMES
an hour is a blink
a *flash*
a wink, a flicker
a dashing gallop


and sometimes
an hour  s t r e t c h e s

**238**

thuddingly
    second
        by
            second
                by
                    slow
                        second
an endlesssssssssssssss
eternity
of
    d
    r
    i
    p
    s . . .

As we waited for Mom and Dad
to return from Mrs. Falala's
time was not galloping.

It was d

r

i

p

p

i

n

g

so painfully
slowly.

# NOTEBOOK

We sat on the porch steps.
We climbed the maple tree.
We tried to fix the broken gate.
     Hammer hammer
     oops
     never mind . . .
We made our beds and cleaned our rooms.

Drippppppping time . . .

*Want to see something?* Luke asked.

From his yellow notebook
he pulled out a crumpled piece of paper.
*Know what this is?*

It was a pencil drawing.
*Some sort of animal?*

*It's supposed to be a cow,* he said.

*But you draw better than that, Luke.*
*I don't get it.*

*I didn't draw it.*
*Mrs. Falala did.*

*Oh.*

*It was one of her first tries.*
*She crumpled it up*
*but I found it later and kept it.*

Luke flipped to the back of his notebook
where there was a pocket flap.
He pulled out another drawing.

*Whoa! That's really good, Luke.*
*I'm so glad you're drawing animals now*
*instead of zombies and dragons and—*

*I didn't draw this,* he said.
*Mrs. Falala did.*
*Last week.*

*Whoa!*

It was an elegant drawing
of a Belted Galloway
and not just any Beltie.
It was Zora:
with those inkwell eyes
and that fur-white belt

and that stubborn-sass look
and that flippant tail.

*What else does she draw, Luke?*

*Oh, lots of things now.*
*She draws Paulie the crazy hog-pig*
*and China the cat*
*and Crockett the parrot*
*and Edna the snake*
*and you know those seagulls*
*that are always lining up on the roof?*
*She draws those, too.*

*And she draws the barn a lot—*
*she really likes to draw that barn*
*and she draws the fenced pasture*
*and the house*
*and you know that window way at the top—*
*like maybe the attic?*
*She draws that sometimes.*

*Just the window?*

*Well, yeah, with different things*
*coming out of it.*

*Things coming out of the window?*
*Like what?*

*All kinds of things:*
*flowers and ribbons*
*and stars and leaves*
*and musical notes—*

*—Musical notes?*

*Yeah, like this:*

*Luke, have you ever heard flute music*
*coming out of that window?*

*Sure. Mrs. Falala plays the flute.*

*What? How do you know* that?

*She told me.*

*When was that?*

*One day when we were drawing.*
*I asked her about those notes*
*coming out of the window.*
*She said that sometimes she plays*
*the flute and when the room fills*
*up with the music and has*
*nowhere else to go it floats*
                    *out*
                            *the*
                                    *window.*

*What about the stars and flowers*
*and leaves and ribbons?* I asked Luke.

*Did she say why she draws those*
*coming out of the window?*

*She said that room up there is a*
            *remembering room*
*and when she is up there*
            *remembering*
*all those things fill up the room*
*and when the room is too full*
*they fly out the window.*

*Just like the music?* I asked.

*Yes, I guess, just like the music.*

*So is it always good things*
*coming out of the window?*

Luke put his hands to his cheeks.
*One time she drew lightning bolts*
*and spiders and bats coming out*

*of the window. Very creepy.*
*She was in kind of a bad mood that day.*

Mrs. Falala. So much
we did not know
about her.

**DRIPPING**

D    r    i    p

r

i

p

                    D                   D

                    r                   r

                    i                   i

                    p                   p

D   r   i   p   p   p

r

i

p

p

p

p

Dripping slow time as we waited

and waited

until

finally

we heard

the sound

of

a

car

pulling

into

the

drive.

At last!

## PUZZLED

*Well? Well?* We were all over Mom and Dad like flies. *What was that about? Who is Mr. Colley? Where was Mrs. Falala?*

I tried to read the expressions on their faces. They looked, I suppose, puzzled, more than anything else.

*Did something happen to Mrs. Falala?* Luke asked.

Dad spread his arms. *No one knows. She's gone missing!*

*Missing?* I said. *How could she go missing? And who is Mr. Colley?*

*Mr. Colley is her neighbor and he's also her attorney. He was supposed to meet with her last night, but she wasn't home—or at least she didn't answer the door. He thought that odd, so he went inside—she never locks her doors—but no sign of her. He went back again this morning, figuring she'd have to be up early to feed the animals, but the house was still dark and still quiet and no sign of Mrs. Falala.*

Mom was gulping down a cup of coffee. *Reena, do you and Luke have any idea where she might have gone?*

The only place I could think of was the fair,

and I said so. *But if she'd gone to the fair, we would have seen her and she would've come back last night, right? And why did Mr. Colley call us?*

*Good question, Reena. I asked the same thing,* Mom said. *Apparently, Mr. Colley knows all about you and Luke helping out over there, and our phone number is written in three places in her kitchen. But right now we need you to go back with us and tend to the animals and have another look around—maybe through the pastures in case she went out walking and fell down or something.*

And so we did, we went back to Mrs. Falala's, in search of her.

# THE SEARCH

Mr. Colley was a short, square, bald-headed man, and I recognized him. Several times in the past weeks he had stopped in to see Mrs. Falala, and each time, he had brought something: a basket of vegetables, a pot of soup, a stack of folders, even a bucket of crabs once. On this day, he was in the barn, along with Mr. Birch and Zep.

*Just checking the barn one more time,* Mr. Colley said.

The animals were agitated, mewing and mooing and squealing and squawking. I went straight to Zora, who was complaining loudly:

*Moooooo    moooooo    mooooooooo.*

*There, there, Zora girl, it's okay, shhh.* I gave her water and filled her grain pail and combed her back. *There, there. Where is she, Zora? Mm? Where's Mrs. Falala?*

*Mooooo    moooooo    moooooooooo.*

Zep joined me in Zora's pen. *I didn't think to check on Mrs. Falala when we brought Zora and Yolanda back yesterday,* he said. He put his hand on my shoulder. *I should have told her how good you did with Zora at the fair.*

*Aw—aw—*

*And how good Zora did, too. Well, after that first
jumpabout!*

I wanted to kiss that Zep boy, right there in
the barn.

The grown-ups headed out to the pasture and
fields while Zep, Luke, and I tended to the
animals. Zora seemed to want extra attention,
nudging me with her big head, nuzzling my
arm.

**Moooooo moooooo mooooooooo.**

Paulie settled down quickly once Zep dumped
some slop in his trough; the cat picked at her
food petulantly; and Crockett kept squawking
even though he had ready access to his seed
and water all the time.

We were about to join the others out in the

fields when I happened to look up at the house, at that third-floor window. It was wide open.

I called out to Mr. Colley: *Has anyone looked in the attic?*

*What?* he said. *The attic? Never thought of it.* He must not have thought that sounded promising because he turned back to his trek across the pasture.

Luke seized my arm. *We've gotta, Reena, we've gotta check up there.*

Zep offered to go with us, so the three of us went inside the house.

*I don't know about this,* I said. *Mrs. Falala might be mad if she found us prowling around her house.*

*But,* Zep said, *she might be grateful if she was*

*injured and needed help and was waiting for someone to find her.*

Mr. Colley had said he'd already checked the rest of the house, so I suggested we go straight to the attic. It was eerily quiet inside. The rooms were sparsely furnished with old but comfortable-looking sofas and chairs and dark wooden tables.

On up we went, up the central staircase, and down a long hall, with closed doors on either side. Not knowing which might lead to the attic, we opened each one: a bedroom that looked like it must be Mrs. Falala's, as her clothes were folded on a dresser and a stack of books and a water glass were on a table beside a made-up bed; next, a storage room, with boxes and suitcases; and a third room seemed to be a guest room, with its simple bed, table, and dresser.

The last door opened on a flight of stairs. We all stood at the bottom looking up.

*Mrs. Falala?* I called. *Mrs. Falala? Are you up there?*

Silence.

Up we went: me, then Zep, then Luke.

The room was smaller than I expected. Standing at the top of the stairs, I could see it all: the desk and bookshelves and table on the left, the open window in the middle, the cot at right, with Mrs. Falala lying on it, her eyes closed, her hands folded around a silver flute.

*Shh,* I whispered to Zep and Luke. I went closer.

*Mrs. Falala? Mrs. Falala?*

It was warm in the room and the breeze from the window was welcome.

*Mrs. Falala? I don't want to frighten you, but— but—* I touched her arm lightly. *Oh. Oh.* I looked up at Zep and Luke and felt so utterly sad.

Luke came up behind me and patted my back. Then he leaned over and patted Mrs. Falala's hand. *It's sort of stiff,* he said.

Zep said, *I'll tell the others.*

*Thanks. We'll wait here.*

I didn't want her to be
alone
in the room
at the top of the house
with her silver flute.

## PORTRAITS

While Luke and I sat quietly beside Mrs. Falala, waiting for the others, Luke whispered, *Did you see what's on the walls?*

Dozens of drawings were tacked along the walls: renderings of the barn, the house, Zora and Paulie and Crockett and China and Edna, the pasture, the fence, the trees.

*Did you see the ones of us?* Luke asked. There were several sketches of Luke, all of him sitting on a hay bale drawing. Two drawings showed me and Zora: in one, Zora was pushing me over with her big head; and in the other I was resting my head along her back, staring off into the field.

Mrs. Falala must have tacked them up in the order she finished them, because at the far left, the drawings were primitive and awkward, but you could see her skills improving as you scanned the room, for the ones at the far right, nearest her cot, were more detailed and fanciful, even playful. On the table was her drawing pad with two final sketches on it. One was of me holding a show stick in one hand and Zora's halter in the other, both of us looking at each other, with blue ribbons floating in the air all around us and a big plop of manure behind Zora. The other drawing was of Luke and me, as we were riding away on our bikes, and trailing behind us were all the animals—

Zora and Yolanda, China, Crockett, Paulie, and seagulls flying circles over our heads. Very small in the bottom right corner was a little figure with a long braid, her hand raised in the air.

## MRS. FALALA'S GIFTS

According to Mr. Colley, Mrs. Falala had spent the past month "getting her affairs in order." This included making out a will, which she and Mr. Colley had finalized the week before the fair.

*She must have had a sense about things. Old people do, you know. After all, she was losing her sight—*

*She was?*

*—yes, yes, and fell a few times—*

*She did?*

*—yes, yes, and she was feeling so weak—*

*She was?*

*—yes, yes, but for the first time in a long while, she had stopped worrying about what would happen to the animals if she died. She must have been looking for just the right family and—along you came.*

*Us?*

*Yes, it's here in the will. She wants you to have the animals.*

*Us?* Mom repeated.

*The animals?* Dad said.

*Yes, yes, the cow, the pig, the cat, the parrot—*

Luke said, *The snake?*

*Oh, is there a snake, too? Well, yes, I suppose—*

Dad said, *But we don't have a farm. We can't take care of the animals.*

I hadn't cried yet about Mrs. Falala's death, but I cried then, thinking of her and of what would become of her animals, Zora especially.

*Maybe you could buy this place then,* Mr. Colley said.

Mom and Dad exchanged a look. I knew that look.

*We can't afford this place,* Dad said. *It's a great idea, but I'm still looking for a job.*

*Oh,* Mr. Colley said. *Oh, I see.*

## MORE DRIPPING

When we left Mrs. Falala's that day, we were all feeling low and blue. Luke and I took turns weeping and staring out the windows. We all took naps. We wept some more.

The
    d  r  i  p
    r
    i
    p
      of the rain
      matched our

d
r
i
p
p
i
n
g
  eyes

and our

        s a  g
              g i n g
                    souls.


And then I had an idea.
It is strange how ideas can arrive
out of dripsagging blue.

*Come on, Luke,* I said. *Let's go find Mr. Colley.*

**270**

## THE PROPOSAL

We found Mr. Colley sitting at Mrs. Falala's kitchen table, reviewing documents.

*I am glad to see you,* he said. *Do you think you and Luke and your friend Zep can feed and tend the animals until I arrange for someone else to do it?*

*Sure,* I said. *We'd be missing Zora so much if we couldn't do that, right, Luke?*

*Right.*

*Mr. Colley? Your property is next to this, isn't it?*

*Yes, over there, the house with the blue door.*

*And wouldn't you like to have more land?* I stood by the window looking out. *All that nice pasture? And that little pond? Mm?*

Mr. Colley joined me at the window. *It is a nice piece of land,* he agreed.

We talked a little longer and then Luke and I fed the animals again before leaving. The following day, Mr. Colley phoned and talked to Dad.

*I have a proposal,* he said. *Let's talk.*

## SIX MONTHS LATER

It is hard to imagine that it was less than a year
ago that we first thought of moving to Maine,
and now here we are, at home in the house on
Twitch Street, with a blizzard raging outside
and a fire roaring in the fireplace, and animals
warm in the barn.

Mr. Colley bought Mrs. Falala's place
(*An investment!* he said)
and hired Dad as the live-in manager
and we all moved here in September.

273

We had a summer of cows and fairs
and "lobstahs" and ocean
and riding our bikes up and down
the narrow roads of this coastal town.

We had an autumn of dazzle-dazzle leaves
red and orange and yellow
and going to a new school
and meeting new friends.

We've had our first Christmas here
and our first blizzard
and our first power outage
and many, many shovelings of snow.

And for five months now
thanks to Mrs. Falala
we've had the company of Zora
and Paulie and China and Crockett
and probably Edna the snake
(who we hope is hibernating)

here on Twitch Street.

Yolanda is also here and Zep visits daily.
*Is he coming to see Yolanda or you?*
Dad asks regularly.
I don't answer that question
because I don't know the answer.

From a file Mrs. Falala kept on her cows,
I learned about Zora's lineage.
She did indeed come from a long line of
### *champions*
and maybe one day when I show her
at a fair
she will receive a blue ribbon
or become a Grand Champion
but
right now
I have a lot more to learn
about showmanship and
about Zora—

that stubborn, crazy, belligerent
sweet, sweet heifer.

Maybe she will calm down
just enough
to please the judges
but not calm down too much—
because then she would not be
Zora.

Luke drew a portrait of Mrs. Falala
with her long white braid
swinging over one shoulder
and he hung the drawing in the barn
so the animals could see it.

We have kept the attic
pretty much as Mrs. Falala
left it: all the drawings on the wall
and her silver flute on the cot
and sometimes Luke and I go up there

and remember her
with her long braid swishing
and her stars and leaves and
music
  floating
            out
  the
        window.


It feels a long, long way
from the city with subways and monuments
and traffic and sirens


to this town
where the mountains
            meet
                  the
                        sea
where people hike and bike
and fish and farm

and to this house and barn on Twitch Street
where we live with animals we love
even
Edna
the
snake
but most especially
with
that
Zora:

That cow!

*Mooooooo.*